Black Loon Lake

S.L. Coelho

Edited by Erin Potter, Shamrock Editing.
ISBN: 978-0986842474

For the hardworking tree-planter,
your work is important to us all.

An isolated lake where the mournful loon calls home, a
place you should not wander off on your own.
In the back country where wilderness always comes
first, there are dangers ever anxious to quiet the thirst.
What happens to some is a mystery to most, but the
wild forever will play the host.

S.L. Coelho

{ 1 }

DID YOU GRAB THE COOLER?

"Yes, honey." The fisherman waggled the blue box in front of his wife.

"Well, I don't want to forget it, or risk attracting a bear."

"Don't worry, the dogs would scare off a wild animal." He put his arm around his partner. He loved his wife, and enjoyed the time they spent together. The relationship was easy, they shared mutual interests and no one else was as tolerant of his bad jokes, as she was.

"Speaking of the dogs, why don't we hear their usual ruckus?" She turned to her husband, her face pinched.

"They're probably napping."

The two older German Shepherds spent much of the day asleep, under shade, to combat the heat.

The couple rounded the curve on the moss-covered path, the dense brush and stunted pines opened up to a small campsite.

They stopped mid-stride. Their campsite had been trashed. The windows of the small camper trailer were smashed. The aluminum siding dented, there was blood, a lot of it. The dogs were nowhere to be seen. All that remained were a single collar, the chains which once secured them, and several tufts of black hair.

The fisherman dropped the contents in his grasp and raced toward the scene. His wife stood motionless, her feet unwilling to carry her forward. Bile burned the back of her throat. The condition of the campsite told her everything; her husband would never find the dogs, their beloved pets met a savage end.

†

The climate, of the Cariboo-Chilcotin region in British Columbia's Central Interior, had scorched flora and fauna since the middle of June. The area hadn't seen as much rain as the South coast, but still held its own kind of beauty; the rugged, wild country was filled with Cedar, Hemlock, and Pinegrass. There were also rattlesnakes, grizzlies, and cougar. It was easy to ignore the risks against the back drop of the majestic glacier mountains with their riot of color, from the blue Lupine, red and pink Paintbrush, to the yellow Brown-eyed Susans. The graceful sway of the wild sedges added to the tranquil environment, which would be perfect, if not for the bird-sized insects.

"Damn it!" Lori slapped her face.

"Another one?" Aaron slipped the seedling into the hole created by his shovel and stomped the microsite down. "That one looks like it's starting to swell."

"Here, let me take a look," Mike dropped his planting tool to examine his girlfriend's face. "It's not too bad, just don't scratch. Got any Benadryl in your fanny pack?"

"Yeah, I think so. I might top up on more Deet too, if you don't mind?" Lori handed Mike the repellent and made a slow turn as he covered her with the spray.

"Thanks. Bloody mosquitos, they're as big as the jays out here. Maybe they should become the provincial bird."

The three planters were on contract with a large tree-planting company. Their progress was slow in this cut-block due to the thick slash, and steep terrain. The stifling heat, which had only just begun, did nothing to ease the burdensome work. Their planting bags were heavily loaded, and the straps dug into Lori's sunburned skin. She worked her fingers underneath the padded material to massage her shoulders. Mike smiled at her and returned to his line.

Mike and Lori were fourth year veteran planters who became a couple in their second year. As a hiballer Mike was one of the highest earners in the outfit. A good planter could plant over 2000 seedlings a day, at eight to \$0.25 per tree; it was a decent day's pay for hard workers. Aside from the physically grueling work, there were down-sides; insects, cramped living quarters- often shared, and privacy was at a premium.

As a rookie Aaron shared a tent with Mike and Lori since the beginning of the spring season. The three had become fast friends. The task of showing newbies the ropes fell to those who had at least one season under their belt. Eventually, Aaron would be partnered with someone else, or more likely, contracted to plant his own cut-block.

Learning to plant takes time, there are strict quality and density requirements. Planters are paid by the tree, not by the hour, and there is a right way and wrong way to plant a seedling; there is no pay for a poorly planted sapling.

Aaron wiped his brow to keep the sweat from stinging his eyes. "Man, I'm looking forward to tomorrow."

The bright sun made Lori squint. "Yeah, I'm looking forward to the time off." She looked at Aaron and gave him a tight smile.

The group planned to head up to a nearby forestry campsite for a few days of much needed R-n-R.

"Okay, who's up for a challenge?" Mike threw down the gauntlet.

"Are you nuts? No way! Half my fingers are duct taped as it is." Lori's silver-sheathed digits reflected the sun's rays, making her fingers weep with perspiration. The tape kept slipping off, revealing raw blisters.

"What the hell." Aaron never backed down from a challenge. "Okay, I will," he was cocky for a rookie. "What's the wager?"

Mike knew it took a whole season to get the knack of planting a seedling quickly. "How about the loser buys the beer for camping?" Mike grinned. This will be too easy. Not only would he make more money than Aaron that day, but he'd get him to buy the booze.

"You're on."

Both men bent low, the only sound was the slice of metal against rock or the crunch of a root. Lori watch Mike then shifted her gaze to Aaron, she shook her head and carried on at her own pace. She wasn't slow, but she was more meticulous than Aaron. I hope he doesn't buy the cheap stuff. She grinned.

Something caught in her peripheral vision, she turned and froze. Yards away stood a tawny cougar. Its gaze fixed on Lori, the cougar's hide shuddered at the withers, the tip of its tail twitched; it was ready to make its move. The animal took a step forward then halted when it made eye contact with the girl.

"Guys," panic rose in her gut. "Guys. Stop!" she said louder. She remembered to keep her voice calm, and never dropped her gaze from the big cat.

"What's the matter now? Another bug bite you?" asked Mike.

"Not exactly. Will you just please stop?!"

The men hauled up, and finally turned around to see the object of her alarm.

"Shit," drawled Aaron. As a city kid from Toronto, he had never seen a cougar before. He was out here in the backcountry of British Columbia for the same reasons Mike and Lori were. He needed money for tuition, and thought he would work on his tan at the same time. Aaron's fantasy of a great tan was dropped after the first week. Now, he wondered how he could match the strange dark segments on his forearms and legs to that of the stark white skin protected by gloves, boots and t-shirt. At least in camp everyone looked the same – like they had dipped their extremities in white paint. His vanity suffered when he went into town – people never looked him in the eye when they spoke to him, they were too busy staring at his hands.

"It's okay." Mike moved slowly and made a downward motion with an open hand. He and Lori had encountered cougars before. "Don't appear afraid. Remember, whatever you do, don't..."

Mike didn't get a chance to finish. Aaron's adrenaline kicked in, he dropped his shovel and planting bags, and began to run, setting off the cat's predatory instinct. A blur of brown bolted after him.

"Dammit!" Mike cursed under his breath then yelled. "Stop! Turn around, make a lot of noise!"

Lori broke into a dead run towards the cat, yelling and waving her shovel. Mike joined in. Aaron soon realized his mistake and what Mike and Lori were trying to do. He stopped, turned around, then shouted and waved his arms like a broken windmill.

Mike cupped his hands, and yelled, "Make yourself bigger! Stand on your toes, bellow, make plenty of noise!"

Aaron did as instructed. As Lori and Mike advanced on the bewildered predator, it paused and broke off the chase, then darted into the dense bush.

"Holy shit! I just about crapped myself!" Aaron said, shaking visibly.

A breathless Lori reprimanded him, "We were lucky it didn't grab you!" She slumped down into the slash and wrapped her arms around her legs.

Mike nodded. He was bent in half, hands on his knees, trying to catch his breath.

Aaron furrowed his brow, "What do you mean?"

Lori leaned back, her face cast to the cloudless sky. "There'd be no way it would want to release its prey."

Mike shook his head. "Don't you remember any-thing from your safety training?"

"Yeah, some," Aaron shrugged.

Mike twisted his head to look at his friend. "If you'd kept running, that cat would have taken you down. You wouldn't have stood a chance."

Lori's eyes connected with Aaron's. "We would've been forced to fight for you. Not a good scenario."

"Oh," Aaron's gaze slipped to the scuff on his boot.

"I guess that was pretty stupid, huh?"

Lori smirked. "Instead of 'Aaron-the-Arrogant', you would've become 'Treats-on-Feet'." Her eyebrows flicked, and she smiled.

"Yeah, well," Mike said, straightening up, "it doesn't look like it's coming back, so let's finish this. Remember, you're buying."

He removed his glove and used the back of his hand to wipe away the spittle from the corner of his mouth.

Aaron trotted back to retrieved his gear. "No way dude, I got this." He bent down and planted a seedling before Mike donned his gloves and stomped the shovel into the ground.

The day wore on, and soon the small group had put in eleven hours. Aaron was close to Mike's time, but his technique still needed work. There were several trees for which he wouldn't be paid. It appeared he would be buying the beer after all.

Black Loon Lake

†

The morning emerged cool, and dew covered the ground. The crew was prepped and ready to take off early. They jumped into Lori's GMC Tracker; it was a tight fit, but with 4-wheel drive, the small vehicle would get them where they wanted to go. Aaron brought a tent, and Mike offered to buy the food, but first they'd make a quick stop in the small town, and then they would be off.

"That'll be $113.57. Cash or debit?" The Indian cashier's brilliant, blue turban was in stark contrast to his worn shirt, which sported slight perspiration stains. He pointed to the 'No Credit, No Cheques' sign and held out his hand. Aaron waved over the cases of beer, and shook the Maxim magazine clutched in his hand in front of the cashier's face. "What?! For this?!"

The man lifted his shoulders, his ennui evident as he recited a hackneyed line, "I don't set the price; I just sell the stuff." He held out his hand once more.

"Son of a...." Grumbling, Aaron dropped one hundred and twenty dollars on the counter and waited for his change.

"Hey!" he yelled in Mike's direction. "You 'bout ready to head out?"

Mike watched the morning news on a TV mounted in the corner of the store. "Uh yeah, just a second. Did you see this?"

Aaron turned around. The anchorwoman reported on an escaped convict from Alberta. "Daryl Reginald Bradford, age 37, is wanted for fraud and sexual assault. He has been labeled as a high risk to re-offend."

Mike reached up and turned up the volume. The perfectly-styled anchorwoman's voice cut through the silence. "He was last seen in Cochrane, Alberta, four days ago, and is believed to be in British Columbia. Bradford has a history of violence; he has been known to break into vacant cabins. If you see this man..." A photo of an unkempt man flashed on the upper left corner of the screen. "...do not try to apprehend him. Call 911 or the local RCMP detachment."

Mike reduced the volume and turned to Aaron. "Why do these assholes always come out here?"

Aaron shrugged. "Look around, dude, it wouldn't be difficult to disappear here." His hand motioned to the window. "There's thick bush, trees, and the forest goes on for miles!"

The clerk nodded.

Mike plunked his purchases on the counter, "Yeah, stupid question. It just pisses me off, that's all."

"Look at it this way. If the cops don't catch him, some cougar will probably have him for lunch."

Mike grinned. "Better him than you right?"

"Humph." Aaron flipped through his magazine.

The clerk tallied the order and bagged the goods. Mike gazed out the window. Lori waited in her vehicle;

it was hot, she had the windows rolled down, her bare leg hung over the driver's side frame, she wore hiking boots and a cap pulled down low over her brow.

Mike watched as she teased and pushed the gum in her mouth around with her tongue, it made subtle popping noises; it aroused him. It's been a long time.

He glanced at Aaron who continued to flip through the magazine. The drawbacks of sharing a tent.

$$\dagger$$

Two hours later, the compact SUV turned onto a deeply rutted, sunbaked road which was no more than a cow trail.

"Are you sure this is the right way?" Lori looked at Mike, her head wobbled with every bump while her hands gripped the steering wheel so tight, her knuckles were white.

"Yeah, according to the map, it's about half a kilometer further in." The next washboard in the road brought Mike's head within a fraction of smacking the roof of the vehicle.

"There's supposed to be a lake here?" Aaron looked from side to side; he rose in his seat and turned to look behind them. The vehicle had been swallowed up by brush; the branches scraped against the metal, sounding like nails on a chalk-board. "You're going to need a new paint job after this."

"Naw, this old girl can handle it – she's seen worse."
Lori patted the top of the dashboard and smiled. She
knew her Tracker didn't look pretty, but it ran like a
top, she made sure of it. "Besides," she said, pointing
straight ahead to a small, partially hidden wooden sign
with *Black Loon Lake* etched in dark, worn lettering,
"we're here."

{ 2 }

THE CAMP WAS CLEANED AND outfitted in fifteen minutes. Aaron had a modern pop-up tent which he assembled in five. Lori cleared the ancient, anchored picnic table of debris and set up the small barbeque. Mike unloaded the bags and some of the food. They'd decided beforehand to park the small 4-wheel drive under the shade of some large trees and leave the food in the back.

"Hey, hon? How about a walk?" Mike smiled at Lori and grabbed a blanket from the back of the Tracker. "Want to check out the lake?"

Lori had opened her folded camping chair and was settled in to read a book. She lifted her eyes off the page and looked at Mike, then at Aaron. "What about Aaron?"

"I'm sure he can find something to amuse himself." Mike grabbed his fishing rod, and small tackle box and tucked everything under one arm. "Right, buddy?"

Mike's lips tightened and he nodded, indicating Aaron should agree.

"Uh, yeah dude." Aaron looked at Lori and waved his hand before running it through his hair. "You guys go on ahead."

"See, he's fine." Mike grabbed Lori's hand and led the way down the path before she could protest.

✝

The lake was several metres from the campsite but well concealed with the thick brush. Forestry sites were known for their fishing, their privacy, and nothing else.

The bush opened up to a small beach covered in fine gravel. The calm water shone like a mirror, reflecting the rays of the afternoon sun which warmed the surrounding area. The only sound was an eerie lament of a loon somewhere off in the distance.

"It's so peaceful," Mike said as he wrapped an arm around Lori. Her bare skin was tanned and warm from the sun; he swept his fingers over the mound of her shoulder, and down the curve of muscle in her upper arm. "It's beautiful, isn't it?" He turned to kiss her, but she pulled back and placed a hand on his chest.

"We really shouldn't leave him alone."

Bewilderment clouded Mike's face. "He's a big boy, he can take care of himself," he cocked his head.

Lori folded her arms. "Yeah? Like yesterday? What if an animal comes around again? What then? He's a city boy."

"I'm sure he's fine," Mike eyes narrowed. "What's gotten into you?"

"Nothing. I just don't think it's right to leave him alone. It's rude, that's all!" Lori turned and took a few steps back up the trail.

Mike grabbed her arm and gently pulled her back. "Look, I just want us to have some privacy. It's been a long summer, if you know what I mean." His eyes widened. "I miss you." His expression grew softer, he gave her a gentle smile.

Lori managed a grin. "I miss you too. But he doesn't know this part of the country like we do," her eyes pleaded with him. "I'll make it up to you," she purred. Her hands ran over his chest and down his arms, then she turned and ran up the trail, leaving Mike alone with his fishing rod.

☦

The Seasonal Conservation Field Office showed no signs of life. A single, older patrol vehicle was parked by a small outbuilding. Daryl Bradford was hunkered down in some scrub he hoped did not contain poison ivy. He scratched a phantom itch on his buttocks before swinging his head around like a periscope.

No movement in the small buildings, no smoke, no lights. Looks like my lucky day.

Hunched over, he scampered to the back of the building where he knew he would find another door. He had broken into a camper trailer a few days ago, but in the process had cut up his hand crawling through the small window. The wound bled profusely, but now it was caked up and needed to be cleaned.

Dragging in a deep breath, Daryl peered into the window; seeing nothing, he grasped the knob and turned.

Damn. Locked.

He put his shoulder against the portion of door closest to the jam and heaved. The frame strained and gave an audible crack. The convict held himself motionless and waited to ensure he would not be surprised by an alarm or a sleeping occupant.

Good.

He applied his shoulder again, and shoved the door aside, peering in. He rubbed his eyes and squinted; the day was bright and the building was dark, as his eyes adjusted, he started to make out mottled shapes. Sunlight bled under the front door, which helped to illuminate the office. A broad smile arranged itself on his face. "Let's see what we got here." He sauntered through the small office into the back area and pushed open two doors. The first revealed sleeping quarters with two sets of full-sized bunks, a large closet, and two desks. He picked up the sheets on one bed and screwed up his nose. "Doesn't anyone bother to make a bed these days?"

He threw the sheet over the crumpled pillow, and moved to sift through papers on the nearest desk.

Daryl rummaged through the dressers before he retrieved a foot locker from the bottom of the closet. It had a sturdy lock. "Looks like someone doesn't trust their roommates."

He scanned the wardrobe rack and found a clean shirt. He held up the navy blue police-style short sleeve, shook it out, and squared it against his shoulders. "This'll work. If I'm going to pull this off, I'd better wash up." He placed the shirt over the back of a chair and headed for the open door which he had seen was the washroom. He emerged clean shaven, hair cropped and slicked back. Daryl had found a first aid kit in the cabinet; he cleaned and bandaged his hand, wrapping it several times. He donned the shirt and a clean pair of pants which he found hung up.

Moving to a mirror, he checked himself out. "Well, there," arms akimbo, he twisted his torso and offered his hand to his reflection, "Hello, I'm officer..." He scrunched his brow and turned around. Daryl scanned the desk where he thought he'd seen a name badge. "There you are," he plucked the tag from the desk and pinned it to his shirt. He returned to the mirror and mustered a phony smile.

"Hello. I'm Officer Conrad, how you folks doing today?"

His smile quickly turned into an indulgent grin.

"That'll do, that'll do."

He raided the contents of the refrigerator before heading out to the vehicle. He'd been unable to find a weapon, but it wasn't paramount; the uniform and marked vehicle should be enough to avert suspicion.

In the truck he searched under the frame, the floor mats, and the glove compartment for a magnetic key holder. Nothing! He had wasted enough time here.

He slapped the steering wheel with the heels of his hands and ran his palms either side of it. "Looks as if I'm gonna to have to hotwire you." Within minutes, he headed out onto the local logging road.

✝

At Black Loon Lake, the heat rose in the air. Lori had abandoned Mike at the lake; he didn't follow her back.

When she broke through the brush, Aaron asked, "Where's Mike?"

Lori scowled. "Back at the lake. I knew this was a bad idea."

"You mean you didn't tell him?"

"No, I didn't tell him." She looked down to kick a rock, sending it skittering a few meters away.

"Do you think he suspects something?" Aaron moved closer to Lori and lifted her chin. "I thought you said you would do it before the next season starts? It's only a couple of days away."

She put her hands up in front of her. "I will, I just- don't want to hurt him."

"So now you have a conscience?" Aaron turned away, shaking his head.

"I told you, I don't like sneaking around on him. Be- sides, I'm sure he's become suspicious."

"What do you mean?"

"Well, I made a stink about leaving you alone, yet I had no qualms about abandoning him at the lake." She raised her brow, her mouth twisted.

Aaron folded his arms and tapped his fingers across his chin. "I see."

A moment later, Mike pushed through the hidden trail and threw his fishing tackle into the Tracker and slammed the back gate. He didn't look at either Aaron or Lori. Lori took up her former position in the camp chair and opened her book, while Aaron stood by the tent with his shoulders hunched and hands in his jean pockets.

Mike flashed both of them a saccharine smile and slouched onto the bench seat of the picnic table while he pulled a fallen, stray leaf apart. Aaron retrieved three cold ones from the cooler and handed one to Lori, who didn't look up from her book, but muttered her thanks. He walked over to the table and held out the beer to Mike.

Mike looked up, grabbed the brew, and shook his head. "Sorry, I'm being a jerk. Lori's right; we shouldn't leave you alone out here."

Aaron and Lori exchanged glances. Aaron clinked his ale against Mike's bottle. "No problem, dude. I get it. You want to be alone with Lori." He shot Lori a sardonic look; she blushed and swiveled in her chair so that her back faced them.

Mike laughed, "Yeah, the drawbacks of sharing a tent, you know." He took a pull from the bottle as Aaron eyed him. "But the flipside is," Mike continued, "we met you, and I think we'll be friends for a long time." He slapped Aaron's shoulder, and the young man choked on the amber liquid. "Easy there, you don't have to down the entire bottle in one swig." Mike smiled.

Aaron nodded and pounded back the rest of the brew before retrieving another for them both.

✝

Daryl managed to travel a few kilometers before he heard the hissing sound. He pulled the patrol vehicle to the shoulder, looked in the driver's side mirror and noticed the flat on the rear left.

"Aw, come on!" He rattled the steering wheel in both hands. "Shit!"

He had to get off the road; he needed to find some place to ditch the truck and find a new mode of transportation. Daryl began his life of crime as a youth stealing vehicles before moving on to bigger things, but not once had he changed a tire, a fact he deeply regretted now. Daryl retrieved a map from the glove compartment; it showed all the un-serviced sites in the region.

He checked the GPS and noted he was between two entrances of the horseshoe-shaped Black Loon Lake. The first entrance was seven kilometers from the direction he had just come; the next entrance was 3 kilometers up the road. He looked back at the tire; there was a little air left, but he intended to ride this truck on rims. He needed to get off the road.

☦

"I'm hungry." Lori rooted around in the coolers. "Anyone want a bag of chips?"

Aaron held up his hand. "Yeah, sure."

Lori tossed him the barbeque flavor.

"What about you?" She inclined her head toward Mike. "We've drank a few and haven't had anything to eat. Hungry?"

Mike rocked on his seat and stood up. "Why not? My stomach is growling. We can cook up the steaks later." He stood beside Lori, smoothed her hair, and planted a peck on the top of her head. Her eyes slid to Aaron, who glowered surreptitiously.

"Want to toss the ball around?" Mike threw the football at Aaron who caught it before it connected with his face.

"Think you can handle it?" Aaron whipped the ball back, aiming for Mike's stomach. Mike caught it, but the momentum brought him around in an arc. A few moments later, the men had moved to an open area near the mouth of the road. They had managed a few passes in their cloaked game of *Murderball* before they heard the squawk and grind of a flat tire.

The patrol vehicle eased up and stopped a meter behind Mike and Aaron. The Conservation Officer made an imperceptible movement downward and the vehicle shut off. He stepped out and offered his hand to the men.

"Hello. I'm Officer Conrad." He looked toward the campsite and caught sight of Lori with her nose in a book. With a thin smile he asked, "I was wondering if you could help me out with a small problem?"

MIKE CAUGHT THE LAST PASS and tucked the ball under his arm. "What seems to be the issue?"

Aaron joined Mike at his side.

Daryl gestured to the truck. "I have a flat and my partner is either out of range, or out of his vehicle, because I have been trying to reach him for thirty minutes."

Neither Mike nor Aaron moved.

Daryl held up his injured hand and rubbed the back of his neck. "As you can see, I'm a little hampered, with the bandaged hand and all." His hand wasn't as injured as he made it out to be, but he didn't know where to start when it came to changing a tire. "I'd appreciate it."

"Sure. No problem dude," Aaron moved forward. "I'll grab the spare; Mike, you grab the jack."

Mike studied Daryl's face. He had a sense of *déjà vu*, the officer's features were vaguely familiar, but he couldn't place him. "Yeah, okay." He dropped the ball and brushed past Daryl. "Do we know each other from somewhere?" Mike asked. "You look familiar."

Prison had taught Daryl Bradford to think on his feet. It wasn't survival of the fittest; it was survival of the shrewdest. "Maybe, when you camped out before?" he offered. "My partner and I work this area."

"No, this is our first time here," Aaron said. "We're planters working at a camp north of here."

"Well, that must be it then," Daryl said. "We occasionally check up on you guys, you know, make sure everyone is safe and the environment is protected and all that." He chuckled.

Mike set the jack under the vehicle frame and levered it up. "Must be," he said, keeping his eye on the conservation officer. He knew he hadn't met him at base camp; those guys never checked up on them, but he struggled to place him. Daryl's image lighted like a wisp of memory on Mike's consciousness, barely a flicker, before it disappeared like vapor.

Fifteen minutes later, the tire was changed and lucky for Officer Conrad, the spare was in good shape, but the rim of the original tire was damaged and would need to be replaced. "Thanks guys, you sure helped me out of a jam."

"You're welcome," Aaron said as he tossed the ruined tire into the box of the truck and shook Daryl's good hand. "It wasn't a big deal."

Mike nodded slowly as he thrust the jack and tire iron under the driver's seat; something told him not to trust this man.

The men heard the snap and crackle of the fire Lori made a few minutes earlier. She started up the barbeque, and retrieved the steaks from a cooler when Aaron decided to play host. "We're just about to eat. Care to join us?"

Mike flashed him a look, and turned to the conservation officer.

Daryl smiled. "Let me check in with my partner; you guys go and help that pretty lady of yours," he said, leering at Lori, "I'll be down in a minute." He pulled himself into the truck and went through the motions of a pseudo call.

Half way back to their camp, Mike yanked Aaron over, "What the hell do you think you're doing?"

Aaron pushed him off and straightened his shirt. "Just being friendly. He's a C.O. for fuck sake. Thought he might enjoy a steak and a beer. That's all."

"I don't like him. There's something about him I can't peg."

"Dude, you need to relax, your mind is working overtime."

From behind them came the crunch of footfalls. "My partner is okay, and I told him where I'd be if he needed me, but I can't stay long," Daryl said.

"How about a beer?" Aaron offered an unopened brew to Daryl. "They're good 'n' cold."

Daryl raised his palms, "Thanks, but I shouldn't. You know." He scratched the insignia on his shoulder.

"All right, but if you change your mind." Aaron smiled and handed the beer to Mike.

Mike started to barbeque the meat and took a long swig from his drink while Lori introduced herself to the Conservation Officer.

"So what's a pretty lady like you doing out here, alone with these two?" Daryl gestured to Mike and Aaron.

"Actually, Mike and I live together. We're a couple." Lori saw Aaron's jaw tighten. "And Aaron is a member of our crew."

Mike flipped the steaks while Aaron passed around more snacks. "Yeah, the big guy here," he said, slapping Mike on the back, "thinks he can teach me a thing or two about planting."

"You need to learn more than a thing or two," Mike murmured.

"Is that so? Well, not according to some people," Aaron countered.

Lori scampered to the cooler and grabbed more bottles to pass around. "Are you sure you won't have a drink with us, Officer Conrad?" She flashed Aaron a warning look. "We're supposed to be enjoying ourselves, after all."

"Well, technically it is after my shift." Daryl looked between Mike and Aaron, sensing there was more than a friendly rivalry between the two. "Sure, thank you."

Daryl Bradford continued small talk with Lori. He noted the growing tension between Mike and Aaron and he thought he could use it to his advantage. Lori was in a talkative mood as long as the subject was off the three of them. She talked about university, being a planter, travelling, and what she wanted to do when she graduated. In Daryl's reality, her chatter was incessant; he tuned her out, although he kept up the pretense of a polite listener.

Mike didn't say much; he listened and Daryl noticed Mike was sizing him up, taking in his features. Daryl was confident Mike hadn't figured out where he had seen him before, because a puzzled expression would replace Mike's intense gaze.

"Steaks are up, come and get 'em," Mike said.

Aaron was the first one to the barbeque. "Smells good dude." Mike didn't acknowledge him; he was still pissed Aaron had invited the C.O. in the first place.

"Oh, don't get up. I'll get you a steak," Lori said as she patted Bradford's arm and smiled.

There was still a good deal of sun still up and Daryl watched as Lori sashayed away. There's a broad who needs to be handled, shown who's boss, and when to shut her pie hole.

Aaron sat back in his chair and wolfed down his dinner. Lori returned with two plates and handed one over to Daryl. Mike was right behind her.

"Thank you," he said and looked up at Lori. "It's been so long since I've had a barbequed steak; it smells great."

Mike pulled up short. "What? You don't have a barbeque at the Field Office?"

Daryl realized his slip. "Well, what I meant was, it has been a long time since I've had one that wasn't a piece of charcoal. Neither my partner nor I are very good cooks."

Mike's eyes narrowed. "Uh huh. Well, I hope this meets with your approval."

Daryl nodded.

✝

Daryl's proclamation of not being able to stay long was now into its second hour, and several bottles of lager later, the conversation became a little more intense. He decided to 'poke the snake' and see what would happen. "So, all of you have been friends for a long time?"

Aaron shook his head. "No, we met a few months ago. We share a tent at the worksite."

Daryl was intrigued. "Really?" He couldn't hide the surprise in his voice. "It must make for some interesting moments?" he taunted.

Lori stiffened; she wanted to avoid any conversation about their arrangement.

"Well, you can always find ways to get around that," Aaron said. The liquor had loosened his lips.

"What Aaron means is..." Lori's voice was pinched. "...we all have taken time by ourselves; it keeps us sane." She glared at Aaron, the light of the campfire reflected in her irises.

Mike, bent forward in his chair with forearms on his thighs, had missed the visual exchange, but Daryl had not.

"So you're saying – you two..." He pointed to Lori and Aaron. "...never...?"

"No! They didn't!" growled Mike. "And what the hell business is it of yours what our accommodations are anyway?"

He saw Officer Conrad made Lori visibly uncomfortable. Lori looked around at the men; Aaron grinned and took another swig from his bottle.

Daryl shifted in his chair. "I just find it...interesting. That's all. No offense," he put his hand up in mock surrender, "it just seems to me you're all pretty cozy with each other, and I thought it was a little...strange. But hey – you're best friends right?"

Aaron guffawed, "Not exactly."

Lori pleaded, "Aaron...don't."

Daryl was amused. He was right, there was something going on, and all he had to do was stoke the furnace a little and the rest would take care of itself.

"So, you're not friends?" Daryl tried to sound confused, but he had a clear idea what had been going on. "Sorry, I don't get it," he said.

"Shit, you get more than him," Aaron said pointing to Mike.

Mike focused on Aaron. "What are you talking about?" he hissed.

"Aaron, don't! Please! I told you I didn't want to do it this way." Lori was near tears.

"No! I'm tired of waiting." Aaron stood up and gestured to Mike. "Hell, the only reason he hasn't figured it out is because he believes you love him too much to do anything to hurt him." He rolled his eyes.

Mike stood up, and hauled Aaron up by his shirt, balancing him on his toes. "What exactly are you saying?" he growled.

Aaron squirmed in his grasp. "I'm saying I've been shaggin' your girlfriend for weeks now," Aaron spat.

Mike didn't release him, but turned to look at Lori.

She began to cry.

✝

Mike's anger ignited like a powder keg, and with his free hand he clocked Aaron in the side of the head, sending both of them tumbling away from the campfire. Aaron regained his footing first, but Mike scooped out Aaron's legs from under him with a well-placed kick. Mike jumped at Aaron, but he was too quick and rolled away, and it was Mike who was pinned on his stomach. Aaron delivered a couple of punches to Mike's ribs. Mike bucked and twisted an arm free, which he

wrapped around Aaron's neck and pulled him down into a tight head lock. With Aaron parallel to him, Mike began a relentless pounding of his fist into
Aaron's solar plexus.

Lori screamed at both men to stop, but they ignored her. Taken over by adrenaline and testosterone, breathless and in pain, they had become combatants in a bizarre, liquor-infused, territorial dispute. Daryl was pleased to see his divide and conquer plan had succeeded.

"That's enough!" Daryl yelled. He kicked between the two contenders until they curled up in defense. "Don't make me fine you. All your thrashing about the campfire could have started a wild fire." Daryl had his hands on his hips, trying to look authoritative.

Lori nodded, and Mike wiped the blood from his split lip. Aaron dabbed the cut over his eye which swelled up fast.

Daryl said, "I think I should leave and let you work this out yourselves."

Mike waved him off. "It's okay, we're done." He stood up and jerked his chin to the side. "You can leave."

Daryl took it as his cue to back off, "All right." He eyed the trio, confirming they were still rattled. "Sorry the evening ended this way. Thanks for dinner."

He turned in the direction of the patrol vehicle and slowly made his way back while straining to hear the conversation. A smile was plastered on his lips. He would be back.

{ 4 }

LORI REACHED FOR MIKE'S LIP, but this time, it was he who pulled away. Aaron remained on the ground; Mike turned and walked toward the little 4x4. He couldn't leave; Lori had the keys in her pocket. No matter how angry he was, he wouldn't take the vehicle and abandon them, but he couldn't stick around either. He needed to cool off.

"Mike, wait!"

Mike ignored Lori's plea; he retrieved his jacket and a flashlight from the SUV and slammed the door then headed toward the lake. Dusk had settled.

Lori caught up to him and grabbed his arm. "Please, wait. Let me explain."

Mike shoved her off and continued to move forward.

"Mike, don't go. I love you!"

Aaron looked at Lori, shook his head, and chuckled.

Mike flipped her off. "Screw you!" Then he stopped and turned to face her. "Oh wait, Aaron already took care of that, didn't he?" His eyes penetrated into her skull. He wanted nothing more to do with her. She betrayed his trust and his love; he was done. He turned and was enveloped by the brush.

Lori stood dazed, her face streaked with tears.

Aaron came up behind her. "Well, at least it's out in the open."

Lori wheeled around, a venomous look shrouded her features. She slapped Aaron across the face. "You asshole, he didn't have to find out this way!" She stomped off toward the tent.

"I thought you wanted him to know," Aaron said, holding his cheek. Lori's strike had left a welt on his face. "Whaddya doin'?"

She ripped her sleeping bag and backpack out of the tent. "I'm sure as hell not sleeping in there with you," she said as she pushed past him and threw her things into the front of the Tracker, then made up a bed in the backseat.

Aaron stood stunned.

Lori backed out of the vehicle and turned on him. "In fact, I'm never sleeping with you again. We're finished," she seethed.

"He's not going to take you back, you know."

"Maybe not, but I should never have slept with you. You're a pig."

"No. You're a classic, little minx. I didn't have to work at it at all. You wanted me as much as I wanted you."

Lori went to slap him again.

Aaron grabbed her wrist. "Careful." He gritted his teeth. "I won't take it a second time."

"Fuck you!" she yelled and jerked away.

Aaron smiled. "You already did, sweetheart." He turned and schlepped back to the tent.

During the fall-out, no one noticed Officer Conrad had only backed the truck up a short way down the road. It was concealed from the campsite at this distance; he had left the lights off and returned to watch the exchange. He wrung his hands, and his breath quickened. "Don't worry, I'll show you how to behave. You need to show a little more respect for a man."

Daryl sneered; he couldn't wait to put Lori in her place.

Little bitch.

✝

The full moon illuminated the lake, casting a pale reflection around the shore. Mike carried the flashlight in his pocket. The lake was as still and level as a pane of glass. The only movement was a ripple caused by a lone loon. He didn't know how far he had walked. He made his way around the shore of the horseshoe-shaped body of water, occasionally forced to trudge through the bush where the shoreline disappeared, and later return to the beach when it re-appeared. He had seen on the map there were two entrances to the lake; they had come in on the west side; the east entrance was several kilometers away. All that lay between the gulf of the wide tributaries was dense forest and scrub.

Mike came across a large piece of deadfall which washed up on shore long ago. It was dry and petrified, making it the perfect seat. He parked his posterior on the gnarled piece of wood and tugged his jacket around him. The nights were chilly up here; he could see a plume of fog as he breathed. He noticed a large stone near his boot, he picked it up and rubbed the dirt and sand off it. Worrying the rock, his thoughts strayed to all the times Lori and Aaron had been away from the tent at the same time, or how they just happened to meet back at the tent together. Or, when he would wake in the middle of the night to find Aaron hadn't returned from his poker game, and Lori had left the tent while he'd slept.

Poke-her, yeah right. Clever play on words, Aaron, you prick. Mike ran his hand through his hair and rubbed his scalp. How often did they laugh at me? What a dumb-ass, dip-shit I am.

With three concussive blows, he slammed the rock into the driftwood. "Damn, damn, goddammit!" As his vision misted with tears, he hurled the stone into the lake; it hit the water with a loud *kerplunk,* a loon screamed in the background. His hurt and anger returned. "Why didn't I see the signs?" he said aloud.

In answer, the loon returned a call.

"You're right," he said to his phantom counselor, "because I didn't want to see it. I trusted them. No. I trusted her." His heart ached; he wanted to slam his fist into something to divert the pain. He wanted to scream into Lori's face, 'How could you do this to me? To us!' The couple moved in together seven months before; he thought everything had gone well, he even considered marriage. He realized no answer she could give would satisfy him or justify her betrayal.

As far as Aaron was concerned, when Mike thought about it, the guy was always friendlier with Lori and over-confident with him. Mike never gave it much thought; he assumed it was insecurity on Aaron's part, and he was over-compensating.

The night grew cooler and Mike was exhausted. He would ask Lori to take him into town tomorrow, where he would catch a ride to the work camp and request another crew. It would be granted; Mike would get the cut-block of his choice. When the season ended, he would move out of the apartment.

He wiped his face and took in a deep draught of night air. He decided to head back, though he had no idea where he would sleep; he just knew he needed to before he collapsed. All the strenuous work over the season, the fight, and the booze came together in one collective mass, hitting him hard. He switched on the flashlight and began to make his way back when he heard it.

He stopped. He heard movement in the bush, snuffling and short grunts; his heartbeat quickened. He'd come across bear scat some meters back.

Chastising himself, Mike realized he'd gone out there without precautions, no bear spray, no weapon, not even a damn stick. His safety training kicked in; he had to let the animal know he was there.

Be loud.

He began to sing the only song which came to mind: *Ninety-nine Bottles of Beer*. He rolled his eyes.

What the hell, it's a song.

He sang at the top of his lungs, "Ninety-nine bottles of beer on the wall, ninety-nine bottles of beer, take one down, pass it around, ninety-eight bottles of beer on the wall..." He listened intently as he sang, passing the flashlight back and forth over the brush. He picked his way around the shore until he was several meters away. He stopped singing and listened.

Nothing. Whatever it was, I must have scared it off.

✝

The molding of the plastic door panel protruded through Lori's thin pillow. Her neck was bent at an awkward angle, and her legs ran up the side of the opposite panel onto the vinyl window, in hair-pin fashion.

She was uncomfortable, but she would not sleep in comfort if it meant sharing a tent with Aaron. When she returned to work she would tell the company she won't take the second season; she guessed she would be busy looking for a new apartment, as she couldn't continue living with Mike.

Lori unzipped her sleeping bag and swung her legs down to the floor-mats and angled her body diagonally in an attempt to get comfortable. She was cold, and she had to pee. She fumbled in her backpack for a flashlight with one hand, while donning a sweatshirt with the other. She climbed out of the cramped vehicle, shaking herself out in the first few steps. The tent was only a few meters away; she could hear Aaron's resonating snores.

She shot a disdainful look at the vinyl shelter. "I hope you wake up with one hell of a hangover, dude," mocking Aaron's vernacular.

She noticed the thick, large stick they'd used to push around the logs in the fire pit and picked it up. Along the short trail to the outhouse, she whacked the grass on either side of her as she went. Lori didn't fancy a bite from a surprised snake.

The rank odor was strong; she smelled the outhouse before she reached it. She propped the stick by the door; the paint had peeled long ago and rot ate away at the wood like a cancer, leaving large gaps between the boards. With one hand, Lori moved the blue rays from her light around the entire cavity of the toilet pit, while covering her nose and mouth with the other.

Gross! I'll have to remember to dump the embers from the fire into this hole. It was a trick-of-the-trade she'd learned working in the bush.

Large, black wolf spiders retreated from the illumination, and she made a mental note of where they were.

Geez, I hate those bloody things.

She shuddered, then lifted the lid and carefully inspected the surrounding area before she hovered her behind over the pit, and relaxed. She heard a faint rustle outside and quickly finished. As she stepped out, she flashed the light around and reached for the stick. Her hand groped over the brittle wood; she turned the beam onto the side of the outhouse and the ground around it. The stick was gone.

☦

"Aaron, this isn't funny!" Her heart picked up in its rhythm. "Don't think you're scaring me." She strained to hear the smallest sound. "Don't be an assho—"

She sensed a swift movement to the side of her. The blow across her back sent her sprawling into the dried grass. The searing pain sent ribbons of fire up her neck and down her legs, as her world spun. He grabbed her from behind, his hand twisted in her hair as he pulled her head up and back. With the motion, she was pulled to her side and her eyes locked with his.

Black Loon Lake

His breath reeked of stale alcohol. "Who you callin'
an asshole?"

Lori screamed.

DARYL'S FACE WAS CENTIMETERS FROM Lori's, and his foul breath made her gag. Her pulse pounded in her eardrums; she kicked and scratched at his bare skin.

"You little bitch!" Daryl slapped Lori hard, sending her onto her stomach.

"Aaron! Aaron, wake up!" Her voice cracked with the strain of volume.

Daryl straddled her and held the thick branch across her back, while he clawed and fumbled his hands down her thigh and back up into the leg of her generous shorts. "Someone needs to teach you a few manners." He ran his tongue up the side of her face.

Lori yelled, pitched, and twisted. She snapped her teeth at his face like a rabid animal. "Stop, stop!" she pleaded. "Aaron! Mike!"

Daryl laughed, "No one is coming to your..." His words were cut off when he felt an arm wrap around his neck and drag him off Lori. The stick was loosened from his grasp, peeling a layer of skin off as it was wrenched away.

Lori dug her nails into the dirt and scrambled away, skinning her knees. Her lip bled from the slap and a slight trickle of blood ran down her thigh from Daryl's attention to her skin. She turned to see her rescuer; it was Aaron, shirtless, eyes wild. He wailed on Daryl, pounding him to near unconsciousness.

Wide-eyed, Lori watched in shock as Aaron subdued her attacker, and Daryl sagged in the dried grass.

Lori's eyes met Aaron's. "Thank you," she whispered and stood. "I thought..." Her silent tears came; her shoulders shuddered.

Breathing hard and speckled with blood, Aaron stood over Daryl, his face pinched with concern. "Did he hurt you?"

Lori shook her head. "No, not bad. He didn't get a-"

She felt herself knocked to the ground. The impact forced the air out of her lungs, and she wheezed in a ragged breath.

"Lori! No!" Aaron found himself down in the scrub as he thrust his arm out to grab her.

✝

No one had seen the reflective eyes in the dark, which at first were drawn by the smells of food and blood, but now by the implied threat to its territory. No one saw the silent rush of the huge male bear, not until it was too late.

In its charge, the bear blindsided Aaron with a cuff, splaying him on his back. Its target was Lori, the smallest of the group.

Lori cried out and flailed her arms, encouraging the attack further. The large bear swiped her leg; its claws found purchase in the flesh of her calf muscle and pulled her down. She shrieked and let loose a hailstorm of punches on the animal with ill-effect, while she tried to protect her mid-section. The animal bit down on the top of her skull and dragged her into the bush, leaving a clear swath of blood in its trail.

Dazed, Aaron raced after Lori. He followed the screams until minutes later, all became silent.

"Lori! Lori!" Aaron's sobs went unanswered, his chest heaved, he repeatedly wiped his bruised and battered hand over his face. He paced back and forth between the area of attack and where he'd last heard her scream. The tall, dried vegetation was painted crimson.

How could anyone survive this? There is so much blood.

Aaron dropped, despondent, into the Pinegrass.

✝

Mike continued down the shoreline, his senses on full alert when he heard additional noise ahead. It came from the camp; it sounded like a struggle. Mike leapt into a flat out sprint. He saw in the distance, the glow of the campfire which still burned. His breath came in hard, shallow gasps; the terrain was uneven, and the small, round gravel gave way under his weight causing him to skitter and lose ground. His face was scratched from the odd branch which hung over the trail along the shoreline.

He had come to a spot on the lake where the shore disappeared. It forced him into the brush; it was darker now and he could not see as well as he had when he'd passed this way before. He pushed forward, leaping over fallen trees, and dodging low hanging branches. He was close to the area where the beach opened up again when he tripped over something, and landed face first in the forest detritus.

The spill rattled his brain. The tumble happened so fast he didn't have time to break his fall. He shook his head and spit out the leaf litter which clung to his lips. Scanning the area, he noted a sharp branch protruding from the earth near his stomach. Another few centimeters and he would have been skewered like a pig on a spit. He brushed at the branch, but it didn't move. He noticed it was white, not the typical moss-covered brown. Mike looked back to see what caught him up, and kicked it to reveal the head of a dog, badly mangled, but still attached to its body. The 'branch' was what was left of the dog's hind leg; the carcass had been hidden under leaf litter.

"Shit!" Mike protracted. He stood up uninjured and launched into a run again while he yelled out for Lori and Aaron. He didn't want to surprise the bear that had left the cache, and become a victim himself.

Screams and shouts rung in his ears. "Lori? Aaron?" He listened but received no response. His voice was lost on the wind which had picked up a few minutes earlier. He continued to shout their names, adding, "What the hell's going on? Is everyone okay?!"

Mike crashed through the bush moments later. His eyes took in the camp; it seemed quiet, but closer to the mouth of the campground he saw movement. He jogged over to the grassy rise to find a bloody Aaron, and a barely conscious conservation officer lying in the scrub.

"Aaron, what the fuck happened?" Mike's eyes were wide. "Where's Lori?" His eyes scanned the area.

Aaron stood unresponsive, a vacant stare over his countenance.

Mike grabbed him by the shoulders and shook hard. "Where's Lori?"

Aaron registered recognition and began to whimper, "It took her. I tried to find her, I tried, but it took her." He whipped around, pointed to Daryl, and discharged a rancorous blast. "It's all his fault!"

Aaron advanced on Daryl Bradford once again, but was pulled up short by Mike, "Wait! What do you mean

'It's Officer Conrad's fault'?"

Aaron turned back on Mike and grabbed his fore-arm. "The bastard tried to rape her!" His gaze seared into Mike's face, then softened. "But ..." He sucked in a sharp breath which came out in a shudder. "...it took her dude, it took her!" He jostled Mike before collaps-ing into sobs on his chest.

Mike held Aaron while he took in his words. The full moon illuminated the entire scene; he saw the swath of blood, clear evidence something was dragged away; he heard Daryl moan, saw him roll over and put a hand to his temple. Mike studied the man, filthy, disheveled, and knew immediately where he had seen him before. Officer Conrad was Daryl Reginald Bradford, the fugi-tive wanted for sexual assault, among other things; he had seen his likeness on the television at the store just that morning.

Mike pulled Aaron away and held him by his shoul-ders. "We have to find Lori," he gave Aaron a slight shake. "Are you with me? Can you do this?"

Aaron nodded, "Yeah, sorry, it was just so..."

"I know," Mike looked around his voice unsteady. "I can imagine. Come on, we have to hurry!"

"What about him?" Aaron glared at Daryl.

"I have an idea how to deal with Bradford." Mike trotted over to Daryl and kicked him in the side with his cowboy boot.

"Who?" Aaron's brows furrowed.

Mike hauled Daryl up by the back of his shirt. "Remember, I told you there's something about this guy?" He pushed him toward the patrol vehicle.

"Yeah?"

"Well, I finally know where I remember him from. He's the fugitive from Alberta. Meet Daryl Bradford – asshole extraordinaire."

Aaron lunged for Daryl once more. "You son-of-a-bitch!"

Mike stepped between the men. "Not now, we have to find Lori. I saw some rope behind the seat when I put the jack away. Help me tie this reject up."

✝

They wasted no time tying Daryl up. He shot the men a baneful look and said, "So you're playing hero now, huh? What do you plan to do with me? Turn me in to the RCMP?" he chortled.

Mike gave him an artificial smile. "Not at the moment."

He and Aaron lifted Daryl and unceremoniously tossed him into the box of the pickup truck; his feet were bound and tethered to his hands, which were lashed behind him. His head bounced off the flat tire where he landed with a *thunk.*

"Fuck-heads, fuckin' assholes!" He slammed his feet against the box. "You can't leave me here like this. What if that thing comes back?"

Aaron returned from his tent, shoes and shirt on. "He's making too much noise, we won't be able to hear Lori if she calls for help."

Mike looked around the cab of the truck and retrieved an old rag from the glove box. "Here," he handed Aaron the rag, "shove this in his mouth, and shut him up."

Aaron smirked and rolled up the dirty cloth. "Glad to." He pushed the material deep into Daryl's mouth and gave him a parting boot. "We'll be back for you later," he said and then looked around and flicked his eyebrows, "if there's anything to come back for."

Daryl thrashed about the box, shouting muffled curses, his face red with rage. Mike leaned over the side of the box and held up the stick Daryl used on Lori. "If you don't be quiet, I'll use this on you, and you really will become dinner," he snarled.

Daryl stopped jerking around and backed up to rest on the flat tire.

Mike tossed the stick aside and pulled Aaron along towards the bloodied trail. "Come on. Show me where the...bear...?" His questioning expression was confirmed by Aaron's nod. "...took Lori."

They directed their flashlights over the terrain and around the brush. Back and forth they swung their beams as they raced into the thick bush, calling out for the young woman.

Daryl fumed in the box of the patrol vehicle. He slipped on the cold metal, and the grooved humps dug into his ass; he wriggled his way up the tire sidewall once more, and slipped again. He felt pain run up his arms as something tugged hard at his wrists. The rope had inadvertently caught on the damaged rim.

Daryl smiled. He had literally fallen on his own salvation; he furiously ran the rope over the rim's sharp edge.

{ 6 }

THE WIND HAD DIED DOWN, but the warmth of the ground mixed with the chill blown in from the lake formed a light fog. The illumination from the flashlights went half the distance it would on a clear evening and slowed the progression of the two men.

"Lori!" Mike cupped his hands to direct the call further. "Hon, if you can hear me, make noise!"

Aaron looked at Mike, his face shrouded in concern.

Lori's disappearance had wiped away the rivalry between them. Mike's voice was tight. "I should never have left."

"It's not your fault. It was my idea to come out here." Aaron's chest felt constricted, his lungs compressed by an unseen weight.

Mike looked at him, "There's plenty of time for the blame-game later." He clasped his hand on Aaron's shoulder which made the other man wince. "Let's find her first – okay?"

Aaron nodded and called out for Lori.

"We should try an area near the lake where I saw the carcass of a dog," Mike suggested.

"A dog?"

"Yeah, pretty gruesome, it's a bear's cache, I'm sure of it; the dog had been covered up like a cat covers litter."

"Okay, lead the way," Aaron shuddered. "I pray she's still alive."

"Don't go there. I'm focused on finding her; I'm not leaving until we do. Understand?"

"You don't have to recruit me; I'm with you," Aaron drew his lips tight.

"Good, let's move ."

✝

The full moon was high in the night sky. They jogged to the place where Mike had discovered the dead dog, they took turns calling out for Lori, but there was never a response.

"Hold up, we're getting close. I don't want to surprise the bear and create a worse scenario."

"Agreed."

Mike called for Lori in a calmer voice, "Hon, if you can hear me, please make a sound, bang something, call-out if you can..." His words caught in his throat;

the mass which formed there threatened to cut off his air supply, he felt the sting of tears. "Please, just be alive. We're coming baby, we're coming," his voice cracked.

✝

They found the dog, and discovered it was actually two. They looked like German Shepherds, but it was hard to tell, they were decomposed, stiff, and flattened. Maggots consumed the underside of the one directly on the ground; Mike had tripped over the one on top.

Aaron covered his mouth. "Let's go, there's nothing here."

They searched the area for hours with no sign of Lori.

Aaron said, "What do we do now?"

"We go back to camp, take the Tracker and drive to the nearest Conservation Field Office for help," Mike said, his jaw set. "We're not giving up on her, but we need help."

Aaron bobbed his head in reluctant affirmation. They quietly worked their way back to the campsite. Two kilometers past the cache, and half a kilometer to the campground, they heard a splash in the lake.

Following the sound down to the shore, they saw the lake rippled in the moonlight. Their eyes strained to see in the dark, but the fog was thicker on the water.

"Lori!" they shouted.

A moment later a loon bobbed up to the surface and warbled.

"Dammit." Mike cursed.

Aaron waved his light over an area of bush by the water; something reflected in the beam. "Over here!" he said as he raced toward the object.

"Careful." Mike warned.

"I found something." Aaron picked up a sodden article of clothing and handed it to Mike.

Mike extended his flashlight to Aaron. "Here, hold the light on it." He held up the garment to see it was Lori's sweatshirt; the University logo shone in the beam of the flashlight. It was torn apart; full of blood, and one of the sweatshirt arms was missing.

Mike's composure abandoned him. "Lori! For God-sake, where are you?!" He slumped to his knees in the damp gravel, his face buried in the sweatshirt.

Both men were still. They knew she wouldn't be found alive, but neither willing to acknowledge it aloud.

"Come on," Aaron said as he pulled Mike up, "we need help, so let's get it."

Mike wiped his eyes with his jacket.

"How do we get the Tracker started? Lori had the keys." Aaron asked.

The men realized their way out was as far out of their reach as the moon. Neither had ever hot-wired a vehicle, they didn't even know where to start.

"We'll pull the wires and keep putting pairs togeth-er until it starts," Mike said.

"What if that just screws us up more? We don't know what we're doing."

Mike's jaw tightened. "You're right, but I bet that scumbag Bradford hot-wired the patrol vehicle. We'll force him to help."

A satisfied glint shone from Aaron's eye. "It would be my pleasure to ensure his co-operation."

✝

They were only a few meters from the Tracker, when they felt a thunderous presence behind them. The burly bear bellowed its declaration as the men sprinted for the small SUV. Mike reached it first, climbing on top of the vehicle to give him the boost he needed to make it up the tree. He knew some bears were excellent climbers, but he also knew the two of them wouldn't stand a chance in the little vehicle with its canvas and vinyl back; their only haven was the large cedar under which it was parked.

"Aaron, run!" Mike stretched out his fingers. "Give me your hand!"

Aaron's legs pumped like pistons; his thighs and lungs burned with effort. He looked over his shoulder. The bear moved with such speed, it was closer than Aaron realized. He leapt at the vehicle, clawing to find purchase and pull himself up. Mike grabbed him by the back of the pants and yanked; they wasted no time scrambling up the tree to find temporary solace in the branches.

The bear's first attempt to climb the back of the vehicle, resulted in the animal going through the soft-top. It huffed and popped its jaws, its body swayed side to side, the muscle rippled under the deep hide. The bear looked up at the men, and walked around to the front of the small 4x4. The massive claws lacerated the metal; the sound made the men wince involuntarily. The bear pulled itself up onto the hood of the vehicle, while its frame protested under the animal's hulking weight.

"Come on! Climb higher." Mike ordered.

Aaron was a meter below him. Mike managed to move up several meters and picked the slightest branch he thought would take his weight. Aaron grasped the branch above him, and brought up his knee to pull himself up.

The bear stood up and clambered up the bottom portion of the tree, securing one paw against a sturdy, low bow. It reached up and swiped Aaron's foot; its claws dug deep and pulled.

Aaron howled and tried to pull himself away with his free limbs. Mike scrambled down and grabbed Aaron's hand and yanked. With every muscle fiber strained to exhaustion, the men shouted at the wild animal. Mike held Aaron's hand fast, his own ligaments stretched to their limit, his face red with the excruciating effort.

Mike shouted an order to Aaron, "Don't let go!"

Saliva coursed down his chin, he groaned with the tremendous exertion, the veins in his neck bulging. Mike's chest seared with every breath, he willed his muscles to pull harder.

The bear escalated its labor and gave a mighty tug on Aaron's foot, pulling him down far enough to bite into his hip.

Aaron screamed; pale and drawn he looked up at Mike. "About Lori..." He groaned in pain, his eyes rolled back in their cavities momentarily, before he briefly refocused and mouthed a single word- *Sorry*. A tear curved its way down his face, and his eyes closed.

Mike screamed and clawed at Aaron. "No! No!!"

The bear gave a final tug and ripped Aaron from his grasp.

"Aaron!" Mike wailed.

He watched in abject horror as the bear secured its victim and dragged Aaron's lifeless body off into the bush by the lake.

Dawn was a couple of hours away and Mike shook violently from cold and shock. He felt removed from his body and believed he was in a vivid nightmare, one from which he would wake, find Lori and Aaron in their respective sleeping bags, all three sharing the same tent.

S.L. Coelho

{ 7 }

D ARYL LAY MOTIONLESS IN THE box of the
truck. He'd heard the furor over by the other
vehicle and turned to afford himself a better
view. He watched in terror as events unfolded; his
cheeks sucked in and puffed out with every breath. He
felt sure he would be next. He'd labored for hours on
the nylon rope and stopped twice for a break. The rope
was not easy to cut through; the tire rim had lost some
of its cutting edge. Searing pain ran up and down his
arms, the skin on his wrists a bloody pulp from the
tight ligature.

That punk had it coming; it serves him right for
hog-tying me like some kind of mongrel.

Daryl pushed himself through the pain and persist-
ed with the task at hand. After hours, with the warm,
orange flare of sun promising to light a new day, he slid

the rope over the rim and felt the snap. An instant release. He was free.

He removed the filthy rag from his mouth, unbound
his legs, and tossed the rope aside. He jumped out of
the box, but his legs buckled under him. The con-
striction of the binding cut off much of his circulation,
his legs did not respond to his brain's commands. It
took him several moments to gain some footing, even
then, his steps were tenuous and unstable. His arms
and hands ached, his fingertips were blue, he could not
close them altogether. They had swelled from lack of
blood flow; his fingers felt like sausages as he struggled
to open the cab door.

✝

Mike did not know how long he lay across the
branch which scarcely held him. He was numb from
cold and the realization he had lost his closest compan-
ions. The sun cast a thin silver rim of light in the east.
Dawn would soon be upon him. He had to find a way
back to safety. He caught movement by the patrol
truck, which now came into focus at the rouse of day.

The son-of-a-bitch is cutting himself loose. He's going to leave me here!

Mike looked around in a panic. He knew the bear
was out there; he assumed it watched him, but he also
realized he would be a dead man if he stayed in the

tree. His only hope of survival lay in the truck on the rise. The one Daryl Bradford had fixed to take off in.

Better to die trying than die waiting.

It took him seconds to scuttle down the tree. He hesitated at the bottom branches, taking in the campground before he leapt to the ground and bolted for the truck. He didn't look back; he saw Daryl open the handle of the cab door, and stretch onto the floor boards. Within seconds, he heard the engine roar to life and music waft from the radio. Mike reached the truck just as Daryl was about to slide into the driver's seat.

He grabbed Daryl's shoulders and tossed him out of the truck. Daryl grabbed Mike's shirt as he fell, bringing both men rolling to the ground near the rear of the vehicle. Mike straddled Daryl and punched him in the face. Daryl brought up his knee and nailed Mike in the groin, sending him rolling away, curled up in agony. Daryl caught sight of the thick stick he had used on Lori; it lay near the truck at the edge of the gravel; he scrambled to seize it.

Standing on wobbly legs, he cracked Mike across the face.

"You fucking asshole!" Mike tried to stem the warm flow of fluid from his nostrils. "You broke my nose," his head swam with pain, his vision clouded.

Daryl tossed the branch away. "It doesn't matter," he pressed a finger to his chest, and then pointed at Mike, "I win - you lose. I'm leaving, and you'll join your friends as dinner." With his middle finger raised, he saluted Mike and booted him in the side with barely a glancing blow, as his legs struggled to right themselves.

He left Mike lying in the grass centimeters from the road out. Daryl placed his hand on the doorframe of the truck; he had one leg in the vehicle when the bear exploded through the tall grass and charged for the fugitive. Bradford didn't have time to react before the large animal was on top of him. He instinctively crossed his arms in front of his face; the bear latched onto a forearm and dragged him several meters away from the truck. Daryl tried to curl into a tight ball, but the bear bit at his extremities, causing the man to yell and fight back. The bear was driven by instinct and its predatory nature. Bradford thrust his hand out and screamed to Mike, "Help! Help me!"

Mike's vision slowly cleared, but his head throbbed and his balance was off. He struggled to sit up as he witnessed Daryl Bradford's final battle. The fugitive lay prone on his stomach as the bear pounded the man with its front paws. The animal's massive form stiffened and hammered into Daryl's back like a pile driver. The man's body pulsed with every pummel. Rivulets of blood-laden salvia bubbled from Bradford's gaping mouth; his vacant, lifeless eyes stared into a void.

I have to get out of here. Come on, get up!

Black Loon Lake

Mike staggered to his knees, the movement caught the bear's attention. Mike realized he would be dead before he could reach the door of the truck if he didn't make a break for it now. He lurched forward, his hands caught the side of the truck box, which he used to steady himself, as the bear raced forward, moving like a locomotive.

Mike scrambled toward the inside of the cab, and grabbed the steering wheel, at the same moment the bear grabbed hold of the bottom of his pants, and yanked him backward. He fell to the floorboards, looking for anything to hold onto; he reached for the accelerator, red-lining the truck as he attempted to free himself.

The engine gunned, momentarily startling the bear. Mike tucked his legs up and pulled back, but the bear advanced and grabbed above his knee, tugging him backwards. In desperation, he clawed at the floor mats and the fabric on the cab seat when he noticed the tire iron under the driver's side. His fingers clutched the cold metal bar, while he tried to minimize the dive out of the truck. On the ground, he kicked the bear in the head with the heel of his free boot.

The large animal roared and released him. He rolled away, but the bear pursued him, using its claws to turn him over like a flapjack. Mike wailed on the large beast with the metal rod, which only served to fuel its fury. The bear swayed around its prey and let loose one final bellow before it would clamp its jaws down on Mike's skull.

Mike saw his last opportunity and took it. As the bear opened its jaws to announce its intention, Mike called upon every reserve of strength he had left, and drove the tire iron up deep into the roof of the bear's open mouth, before crab-crawling backward to avoid being crushed.

The bear shuddered and fell in slow motion, its massive bulk shook the ground as it hit. Mike could see the tip of the tire iron protrude between the bear's eyes. The force of impact when the animal fell, drove the lethal piece of metal home.

He sat for several moments as his stomach churned; knowing he wouldn't be able to keep its contents down. A moment later, he stood and wiped his mouth with the end of his blood-soaked shirt, and hobbled his way back to the truck.

He didn't notice the second set of eyes in the bush. Eyes which witnessed the entire event. Eyes which were learning.

He slid onto the driver's side and slowly closed the door. Minutes later, he was out on the highway back to town, the radio played a last tune before it broke for the regularly scheduled news.

†

The announcer came on. "Reminding all outdoor enthusiasts to be safe and bear aware. Interesting bit of news; a paper by a University of Calgary professor found most of the fatal bear attacks over the last century were due to predatory males who targeted humans," coughing, "as their food source,"

The announcer's co-host said, "That's unnerving."

"I know, and the article went on to confirm bears that have killed at least once, are apt to repeat the behavior."

The co-host piped up, "No kidding? I read an article somewhere, that younger bears may shadow; at a safe distance mind you," a chuckle wafted over the air waves, "the behavior of older bears. Especially, if they've been orphaned. Does this mean this behavior could be learned as well?"

"Well, I can't comment on that, but discovering humans, equal food, wouldn't be much of a stretch for any animal. With all the campgrounds in this province – it pays to follow the advice of Conservation Officers."

"True. So poor mama bear has gotten a bad rap. I always knew males were trouble." the co-host tittered.

"Hey not all of us. Yep, it appears the females are not the usual suspects after all," the host confirmed before breaking into the next set. "To change things up, we have thirty minutes of commercial free..."

Mike snapped off the volume. Several kilometers west on the highway, he pulled the truck to the shoulder, and wept uninhibited.

S.L. Coelho

✝

Ten kilometers from the east entrance, a man turned off the radio. He glanced at his sullen, thirteen-year-old son, giving him a playful slap on the thigh.

The kid grumbled, "Knock it off, okay? It's way too early in the morning." He leaned his head against the window.

The father gave his son a broad grin. "Man, I love it out here."

His son sat up straighter, and tried to appear enthusiastic for his father. "What's the name of the lake again?"

This was his summer vacation with his dad; it was time to catch up and reconnect. He didn't want to be prickly with the man.

"It's on the map, I have it circled. Take a look."

The boy ran his finger down the worn, crumpled paper. "Here it is," he said, pulling the paper up for a closer inspection. "Black Loon Lake." He gave a satisfied nod. "It sounds nice."

His father beamed, "It sure does. I can't wait to see it."

"Me too, Dad."

Black Loon Lake

ACKNOWLEDGMENTS

My sincere thanks to Mikayla Coelho, Lianne Gauthier,
Cathy Churchill, Karen Beauchemin, Jim Westendorf,
Stephanie Gauthier, Mike Coelho, Sandy Parker,
Rich Weatherly, T. James and Magda Olchawska.
Your valuable critiques, patience, and generous
support are appreciated more than you know.
Grateful thanks to Erin Potter, for her eloquent edits
and dedication to meet my deadline.
My deepest thanks to you all.

S.L. Coelho

ABOUT THE AUTHOR

Popular fiction author and veteran camper, S.L. Coelho, enjoys thrilling readers and scaring them 'just a little'.

She grew up in southern Manitoba, entertaining her younger siblings with tall tales. As she matured, these tales blossomed into written works, which piled up in her school locker.

While employed at the Universities of Manitoba, and British Columbia, her written work attracted the attention of researchers, who requested her assistance in writing grant proposals.

Sometime later, she was cajoled into writing reams of documentation for several manufacturing practices and procedures manuals which were utilized to pass ISO certification. Her most recent responsibilities entailed managing, developing, and delivering a preschool literacy program for 'at risk' children.

Her love of books came from her grandparents' small library, where she discovered the vehicle to experience captivating worlds, cultures and experiences. S.L. Coelho resides in beautiful British Columbia with her husband and two youngest children.

She is an unapologetic chocoholic, chai tea consumer, carefree gardener, and a proud member of The Independent Author Network.

You may contact her through Purple Birch Publishing info@purplebirch.com

www.ingramcontent.com/pod-product-compliance
Lightning Source LLC
Chambersburg PA
CBHW020642130626
46552CB00003B/1351